THE DOCTOR IS IN!

Based on the screenplay "Call a Clambulance!"
by Jonny Belt and Robert Scull

Illustrated by Eren Blanquet Unten

A GOLDEN BOOK • NEW YORK

randomhouse.com/kids

ISBN: 978-0-307-97588-1

Printed in the United States of America

20 19 18 17 16 15 14

On her way to school one morning, Oona saw her friend Avi. He was riding his tricycle.

"*Vroom! Vroom!*" Avi said. "Look how fast I can go!"

Suddenly, Avi hit a rock and fell off his tricycle!
"Ow!" Avi cried. "Mommy, my tail fin hurts."
"You'll be okay, honey," said Avi's mommy. "But
we'd better call the doctor, just to make sure."

Oona waved goodbye as Avi took a ride to the hospital with his mommy . . . in a clambulance.

When Oona got to class, she told everyone about Avi's accident. "The doctor will take good care of him," said Mr. Grouper. "He'll probably take an X-ray."

"What's an X-ray?" Gil asked.
"An X-ray is a picture of your bones," said Nonny.

"Do we have bones?" Oona asked.

"You sure do, Guppies," Mr. Grouper said. "Bones are the hard things you feel under your skin. They help support and protect you.

"Without your bones, you couldn't stand up,

jump,

or swim."

"I went to the doctor once," said Deema. "She made me stick out my tongue and say 'Ahhh!'"

"The doctor was checking your throat to make sure it was okay," said Mr. Grouper.

"What else do doctors do?" asked Oona.
"Let's think about it," said Mr. Grouper.

"Sometimes a doctor uses a special flashlight to look in your ear," said Oona.

"And sometimes a doctor will use a stethoscope to listen to your heart," said Gil.

"He or she will probably take your temperature with a thermometer," said Nonny.

"You might have to get a shot," said Deema.
"Shots hurt," said Nonny.
"Only a little bit," said Mr. Grouper. "But they keep you from getting sick."

"Oona, would you like to visit Avi in the hospital?"
Mr. Grouper asked.
"We can bring him a balloon," Molly said.
Oona thought that was a great idea.

The Bubble Guppies lined up, and Mr. Grouper led them to the hospital. They saw doctors and nurses there, and patients who were getting better.

The Bubble Guppies and Mr. Grouper found Avi's room. Avi was in a big, comfy bed. His mother and his doctor were with him.

Avi was happy to see his friends.
Everyone wanted to know how he
was feeling.

"Avi will be fine," the doctor said. "He broke a bone in his tail fin, but we fixed him right up."

The doctor showed everyone Avi's X-ray.

And Avi showed everyone his cast! The doctor had
put it on Avi's tail fin to help his bone heal.

"Who wants to sign my cast?" Avi asked.

The Bubble Guppies took turns signing
their names and drawing pictures on Avi's cast.

When they were done, the doctor said Avi could go home!

"Let's pretend we're sick!" said Deema. *"Bleauuhhh!"*
"Oh no!" Mr. Grouper said, laughing. "I feel sick, too.
Somebody call a clambulance!"

Mr. Grouper stuck out his tongue and turned green.
All the Guppies thought this was really silly, and they
laughed and laughed.